The Substance of Fire

by

Jon Robin Baitz

SAMUEL FRENCH, INC.

45 WEST 25TH STREET   NEW YORK 10010
7623 SUNSET BOULEVARD HOLLYWOOD 90046
LONDON   TORONTO

IMPORTANT BILLING AND CREDIT REQUIREMENTS

All producers of THE SUBSTANCE OF FIRE *must* give credit to the Author of the Play in all programs distributed in connection with performances of the Play and in all instances in which the title of the Play appears for purposes of advertising, publicizing or otherwise exploiting the Play and/or a production. The name of the Author *must* also appear on a separate line, on which no other name appears, immediately following the title, and *must* appear in size of type not less than fifty percent the size of the title type.

In addition, all producers of the Play must give the following credit on the first page of credits in all theatre programs and on all posters:

"Playwrights Horizon, Inc., New York City, produced THE SUBSTANCE OF FIRE Off-Broadway in 1991.

World premiere presented 1990 at The Long Wharf Theatre, N. Edgar Rosenblum, Executive Director, Arvin Brown, Artistic Director."

The foregoing credit shall be easily readable and not less than (a) 12 points of type or (b) 35% of the largest letter used in the Author's billing, whichever is larger.

The Substance of Fire had its world premiere in 1990 at the Long Wharf Theatre,

M. Edgar Rosenblum,	Arvin Brown
Executive Director,	Artistic Director

and workshopped at Naked Angels.

The Substance of Fire premiered in New York City, off-Broadway, in 1991 at Playwrights Horizons, Inc. It was directed by Daniel Sullivan and included the following cast (in alphabetical order):

SARAH GELDHART...................... Sarah Jessica Parker

MARTIN GELDHART............................ Patrick Breen

ISAAC GELDHART...................................Ron Rifkin

AARON GELDHART ....Jon Tenney

MARGE HACKETT ....Maria Tucci

The Playwrights Horizons production was re-mounted in January, 1992 at the Mitzi Newhouse Theatre at Lincoln Center with the same cast.

CHARACTERS

SARAH GELDHART

MARTIN GELDHART

ISAAC GELDHART

AARON GELDHART

MARGE HACKETT

ACT I

Spring, 1987
A conference room, Kreeger/Geldhart Publishers
New York City

ACT II

Three and one-half years later
An apartment on Gramercy Park

THE SUBSTANCE OF FIRE

ACT I

Spring, 1987.

A conference room, Kreeger/Geldhart Publishers, in the Broadway-23rd Street area. There is a conference table, five chairs, some filing cabinets. There are many books. SARAH GELDHART, a woman in her mid 20s, sits reading. SHE smiles, and nods to herself.

MARTIN GELDHART, her brother, late 20s, enters, smiling. HE watches her for a moment, unnoticed.

MARTIN. Whenever I walk into this room, I tell you, I expect some *guy*, you know, with a manuscript to kick me out. Hey, Sarah.

SARAH. Oh, God, hello, Martin. I know. I've always hated this room. Look at all these books. (*SARAH shakes her head, rueful.*)

MARTIN. Miss Barzakian just cornered me in reception and told me that last week Ventrice, that poet? Know him? So he's—he chases Dad down the hall and he says, and I repeat ... "I'll kill you—you-dirty-Jew-kike-bastard, I'll kill you, you prick." (*Beat.*) It wouldn't be so bad if he were a decent poet.

SARAH. The publishing world, eh? So. What do you think of all this?

MARTIN. (*Thinks for a second, simple.*) It's a bore. You know? What're you reading?

7

SARAH. Oh, something Dad's thinking of publishing. It was sitting here. God knows what he—what he's thinking. "Hobson-Jobson. A Glossary of Colloquial Anglo-Indian Words & Phrases." I mean, tell me, Martin, am I out of touch here or will, like, two people buy this?

MARTIN. Well, I mean, please. No wonder, is it, we're going bankrupt?

SARAH. No, but still, I do feel funny being dragged into it, don't you?

MARTIN. (*Cheerful.*) Well, you *are* a stockholder.

SARAH. Right. I was kind of hoping that by the time I flew in, they'd have it all sorted out. You know? When you're actually happy they've delayed the flight? Anyway, I read the manuscript they're fighting about on the plane and, I mean—

MARTIN. It was bound to come to a head, wasn't it? Look—just take a look at these shelves. You can't do it. You can't go on publishing accounts of—look at this: a two-volume tome on the destruction of the Sephardim during the Spanish Inquisition? Reprints of Traven and Pirandello. Firbank? *That's* big. How many Kreeger-/Geldhart books do you see in the stores?

SARAH. Oh please, we don't have bookstores on the coast, Martin. Let me tell you, I went into a Crown or Dalton or something. You walk in. It's like a Burger-King. There're "blips" from the video games ... it's like, "Buy a Coke, getta Book." I said to the clerk, I'm looking for E.E. Cummings. He said, "Self help, second aisle on the left." And I said, "Are you people still in the *book* business, or what?"

MARTIN. So what'd you think of the manuscript?

SARAH. The thing is, the plane was, there wasn't an empty, and so you can't really focus on the—

MARTIN. You're saying you skimmed? Is that it?

SARAH. Hey, you know I hate to read, it's not fair. But actually it seemed funny, the dirty part, the thing with the two guys.

MARTIN. I hate being dragged into this. And I swore not even to come down here. I sat there after Dad called, you know, I hung up and said to myself, "This is their trip, I'm not part of it. Let them sort it all out because I just don't care."

SARAH. Cut to: Here we are. And ...

MARTIN. Of course to say "No, sorry, I can't," is not an option.

SARAH. Yeah. (*Beat.*) Why *do* we come? I mean, because I'm shooting the show, we're doing three shows back-to-back, and I beg them to re-arrange the schedule. Because I've had a summons from Dad. Who said to me, *last* time I was home, "Sarah, how do you actresses remember your lines?" And I go, "What do you mean?" And he said, quite earnestly, "Because none of you are, let's face it now, all that bright, really. Are you?"

MARTIN. (*Smiles.*) Well, he calls me a "gardener's apprentice," whatever *that* is. At Passover he asked me how the tree-pruning business was. I mean, I teach landscape architecture at Vassar, for Christ's sake. Which is silly, but still. (*Beat, peeved.*) They're late.

SARAH. When has Dad ever not kept you waiting? They're in the library with Aaron's novelist. What's his name?

MARTIN. Val Chenard.

SARAH. Val Chenard. It's like the name of a bad restaurant. In Toronto.

MARTIN. Duck, with a pop-tart filling glaze—Val Chenard. (*Beat.*) And how is the show?

SARAH. Better than I thought. It's very hip for children's television. A little too hip, I think, sometimes frankly. And everyone is like, way too thrilled. But still. "Safe-Sex-Tips-for-Tots" *is* a good skit. (*Beat.*) We didn't really do it—a joke.

MARTIN. Yeah well, no. I saw one. We recently got television in Poughkeepsie. You were a caveman's wife. You were singing "When I'm Sixty-four."

SARAH. Martin, can I ask you something? Does anything happen up there? Are you having a life at all?

MARTIN. (*Smiles.*) And do you know of anyone now who has any sort of a life? Today? People sit alone at diner counters eating meatloaf and thinking of Mom. No one has a life.

SARAH. No.

MARTIN. No. I have my orchard, my bonsai. And *they're* fun.

SARAH. Hey, listen. What I have to do is fly right back to L.A. tonight. I have to turn right back around, but let's grab dinner, can we? After all this?

MARTIN. I can't. I'm sorry. I have to get back, I—

SARAH. No, I understand. No, no. Don't say a thing—

MARTIN. But, Sarah, hey, it's only that there just won't be time. Once we get outta here, and then, you know, I'd miss the ten-twenty, and the next train is like, two-o-*seven* or something. And I have to be in Rhinebeck at *dawn* 'cause I'm putting up a windbreak on the Hudson with the sophomores, which is fun. I still seem to get tired, I don't know.

SARAH. Hey, Martin, remember when we were kids, waiting in this room with some awful thing going on down the hall. Mom and Dad screaming at each other.

MARTIN. Are you kidding? Who could forget?

SARAH. And we were royalty. There used to be so many people working here.

MARTIN. There were never very many people working here, sweetie.

SARAH. It seemed like it. Listen, I don't mean to sound like an idiot, but does bankruptcy actually mean there's a day when this whole place folds up?

ISAAC. (*Entering. Wearing a dark suit of impeccable cut. HE has the slightest of accents—Belgian/German, barely detectable.*) It's not that bad. Aaron exaggerates. Hullo, sweetheart, I'm glad you're here—to get on a plane!

SARAH. Daddy?

ISAAC. You know your brother has his little Stanford-Wharton-Mafia-Flow charts he waves in my face and screams.

SARAH. Daddy. What do you think you're doing? (*Picks up book from atop the desk.*) I mean, "Hobson-Jobson. A Glossary of Colloquial Anglo-Indian Words and Phrases"?

ISAAC. So what's the big deal? A dictionary? A *dictionary,* do you know how few people bother to publish 'em anymore? (And I'm not talking, please, about the University Presses for a tax loss.) I've always done a dictionary now and then if it was interesting enough. Hi, Martin. So. My God, you came, huh. Well. Your brother must've been very pushy with you. You always ignore me when I ask you to come.

MARTIN. Always nice to see you, Dad.

ISAAC. So, tell me, did you get the Edmund Wilson I sent you? I never heard from you. The memoirs.

MARTIN. No, I got it.

SARAH. So what is it? You're not bankrupt, I'm not going to, like, find this place turned into Rug City?

AARON. (*Enters. Younger than Martin and dressed more like an ad-exec than publisher.*) You don't think you were rude to Val?

MARTIN. (*To Aaron.*) Hi.

ISAAC. Was I? I don't think so. I was really rather even-keeled, maybe a little blunt, but he virtually spat on the Krasslow manuscript.

AARON. (*With absolute relish.*) Yes, he did, didn't he? But the Krasslow, Dad, is the last word in boredom. Let me tell you, Val is right. These ossified old academic frauds you trot out every couple of years. You knew Val would be openly contemptuous of your Krasslow, and you deliberately maneuvered him into insulting you.

ISAAC. That's simply paranoid. I'm not that clever.

AARON. Yes, you are. I've seen you do it to me. It's something you do. You navigate a conversation into this place wherein not to insult you would be psychically impossible. Hey, you know something? I don't want to get into a word thing with you, Dad. Do you realize he's about to bugger off to Knopf? And they, Father, let me assure, this'll hit the stores by Wednesday or something. They'll publish it in a second.

ISAAC. Nevertheless.

AARON. And reap a hell of a lot of cashola so doing, damn it!

ISAAC. So what do you think of your brother's little agenda to take over the company?

MARTIN. Oh come on, Isaac, you're not serious.

ISAAC. I've seen it fermenting in him! What do you think, I'm a village idiot?

AARON. Please.

ISAAC. Please! A blood lust for profitmaking. You knew the kind of work we publish—and you have this arrogant idea that you could—God knows the lingo you people use—

AARON. You people? *You people*? What is that supposed to mean?

ISAAC. You know exactly what I mean. You wanna accuse me of bigotry toward MBA's, fine, go ahead. You're not working at Gulf and Western.

AARON. Just this morning, he actually asked me if I wouldn't be happier as a sales rep.

SARAH. Oh dear.

(There is a silence.)

ISAAC. The reason the stock of this company has been kept in the family is because I wished to avoid precisely the kind of confrontation we are having now. If Aaron cannot make peace with the mandate by which *my* company is to be run, he should not be vice-president. No company would settle for less. It is unfortunate, sure, I wanted at least one of you here, but perhaps—

AARON. (*Quiet.*) That's very clear, yeah. Thanks. But the reason I'm here, you know, is that I actually value the stock I hold in this house. Do you need to be reminded? I own twenty percent of this place, Martin, a quarter, and Sarah fifteen. And if you continue the course you're on, we will be flattened.

ISAAC. Not necessarily. You don't know that I'm not going to come up with—

AARON. No you won't, and we will be taken over by someone who is in the book business by accident—some real-estate developer dying for a salon, and this town is full of 'em! A lonely guy lookin' for a tax loss, they'll sniff this place out, hey. Simon and Schuster is owned by an oil company, Dad. These people come in, hang new wallpaper and dollar bills before the end of the first day. You're going to leave us with nothing—a dead company.

ISAAC. The Chenard book is crapolla, kiddo, there's no denying that.

MARTIN. Actually, I don't think so.

ISAAC. Ahh, you read it. You have a literary opinion, Mr. Johnny-Appleseed-of-the-Hudson here?

AARON. I sent it to both of them.

MARTIN. I finished it on the train coming down here. I think it's powerful. I cried. I don't know why.

ISAAC. You're a gardener, Martin, please.

MARTIN. (*Smiles at Sarah.*) You can't imagine how much we look forward to seeing you, Isaac. I don't know. It's just the way you make everyone feel so welcome, or ...

SARAH. And hey, please? What's with this "gardener" business, Dad? Your son's a Rhodes Scholar. You're starting to sound like some sort of Fulton fish market thug, calling names. And besides, what little I read of the book, I sort of liked too.

AARON. (*Turns to Martin.*) You like the book? You really do? I thought you would. I thought you might, both of you. It's something, isn't it?

ISAAC. Excuse me. I've made up my mind. I don't need a little shit-ass democratic committee here to tell me, please, you got it? (*Pause.*) Sorry. To talk like that, to lose my temper. I'm gonna publish Louis Fuchold's six volumes on the Nazi medical experiments.

AARON. What? What are you—?

ISAAC. (*Calm.*) Yes, that's exactly what I'm going to do. That I even let you near a ... a ... decision on such a matter is ... You think that I am going to publish some trashy novel by a slickohipster?

AARON. Dad, this is exactly the problem, this is what I ... you just decided this? What am I doing here? Just to balance the books?

ISAAC. Abraham Kreeger, your mother's father, started this imprint to publish serious work that was valuable in the larger world. We've played fast and loose with that mandate and made some bucks, and God knows I don't intend to lose any sleep over *that* I knew how far we had to go in order to grow. Fuck-you money is fine, but now is the time to get back what we lost. And let me tell you— the Chenard book—is meretricious bullshit! I wanted my time back after I read it.

MARTIN. Well, I think you're mis-reading it.

ISAAC. (*A low growl.*) I tend not to mis-read books. I tend to know exactly the lay of the land.

MARTIN. You have no doubts about your judgment?

ISAAC. Not in regard to this matter.

AARON. Then tell me—why have we been losing so much money?

ISAAC. (*Softens, shakes his head.*) Something has happened. The way in which people read. Perceive. There used to be some silence to life. There is now none. Just static, white noise, fireworks, and boredom all around you. We lose money because we do something that is no longer held to be vital, we're a side-thought to life. And now here you come, Aaron wanting to save us from destruction, running around here with your manuscript like some kind of Typhoid Mary. (*ISAAC looks at the manuscript.*) You come to me here with bright-lights-little-people, less-than-nothing, Tammy Yannovitch—a *hydra*—she's not a writer, she's a monster out of ancient Greece come to swallow cultures, lives, whole cities. These kids with eyes like pinwheels, typing out their little baubles of syntax. *This ain't literature. It's a dress.* You don't read this book. You get a nice little, strung-out, anorexic model who doesn't need a lot of covering, and you put it on her to wear to a gallery opening. (*Beat.*) So listen, Aaron, what I'm saying to you is—it's simple—you've never burdened anyone with your editorial ambitions until now. You're doing fine. You've learned a lot. But these are very tricky waters out there. Forget about this. Go back to your ledgers and you'll be fine. Leave the heavy stuff to me, okay?

AARON. You begged me to come into this business. I mean, these two had sense enough to run a million miles. Now you're trying to kill it off. I can't just sit back and—

SARAH. Listen. Please. It's just books. Really. Please. I see this behavior and I know what's up. You feel usurped.

ISAAC. No, sweetie, please, uh-uh, no.

SARAH. Oh yes, no, you feel "threatened." De-balled your his son.

ISAAC. Sweetheart, please, none of your Neighborhood Playhouse psychologizing. I published Willhelm Fliess, while you were at tap class learning shuffle-ball-flap. "Threatened."

AARON. Hey, you know, I'm not gonna argue that this is not a trashy world out there. I mean, come on, but so what?

MARTIN. Aaron tells me if you go ahead and publish the Fuchold Nazi Medical Experiment book, you won't be able to handle anything else on the Spring list except for a couple of the old reprints. Is that right?

ISAAC. The Nazi is six volumes. I can't hold off production. He's been working for thirty-four years. The man practically, he comes to editorial meetings in his casket. Look, we've never been a big house, so now for a while maybe we're a little smaller. It's not a matter of bankruptcy. It's scale. I'll take a reduction in—

AARON. That's really great. You'll take a cut? Have you seen your Visa bills? For a man who has such rigorous standards—

ISAAC. (*Dangerous and insistent.*) Don't! Don't you *dare* to presume to tell *me* how to spend, nobody—nobody has *ever* told me what to do. Nobody. Not your mother, not the banks, and most certainly not my accountant son.

(*Beat.*) Listen. Why are you so certain the Fuchold will not be read anyhow? Do you know something I don't?

MARTIN. (*Gentle, reasonable.*) Maybe you're not wrong. But why not let Aaron run with this. What harm can it do?

ISAAC. A lot, a lot, in ways you can't imagine, it can all slip away, everything.

MARTIN. (*Reluctant.*) The thing is, we've all noticed—you're becoming unapproachable. And it's like you're on some sort of end-run to self-destruct. We don't know what to do. Do you like to know—there's a whole hell of a lot of phone-action. The topic? (*HE gestures at Isaac.*) And it's not unwarranted, it's a *bore,* but it's *not* unwarranted. You worry us. No end. Look at what you've been publishing. That Englishman's book, Jonally—"The Failure of Art and the Triumph of Technology?" A swipe here at Diaghliev and Stravinsky, a sneer at the Bauhaus, and why not knock off abstract expressionism while you're at it just for a laugh? (*Beat.*) I mean it's time for another tack, Pop, 'cause you're starting to come off as some sort of neo-con.

ISAAC. (*Picks up manuscript.*) Uh-huhm, sure, a neo-con, well, may I, I'll just read you a little passage here. (*HE pauses to make sure they're with him.*) "Alter leaned against the bar, mouth open in recollection of those black hands on his jeans. The feeling of release and submission that comes when someone else unsnaps the buttons—and then, the intrusive rightness of the kid's lips on him, surrounding him in the alley—the cold—the heat—and wetness as his shirt is lifted up towards the spire of the

Chrysler building, glowing above them" ... etc, etc. (*HE looks at Martin, triumphant.*)

SARAH. Well, Dad, I don't understand. What's the big deal here? We all know about blow jobs, don't we?

ISAAC. Yes, we know about blow jobs. That's hardly the ...

SARAH. Well then maybe you publish all these politico books because there's no sex in them? They're totally flaccid. This whole thing is about hormones. You need to get out more, is all, Dad.

MARTIN. The thing of it is, Dad, you see, I promised Aaron that if I liked the book, I'd support him. Whatever that meant. Understand? I do like the book. Aaron is your partner. You drew him in, made promises. And you are able to be the fairest man I know. Occasionally. So publish the book and what's the big deal? Come on.

ISAAC. What do you think, I'll be cornered? What do you think I am? I'll be dictated to? (*HE looks around the room.*) What the hell is going on here? *What*?

AARON. I'm sorry, Dad. I don't understand the Nazi obsession. It has silenced me. I mean, what do you say to it? Look at the Spring and Fall lists last year. (*Beat.*) "An Atlas of the Holocaust." Maps. Blueprints. I.G. Farben's structural reports. All of it on acid-free paper with a hand-sewn binding, a Japanese printing, wholesaling at one-twenty-nine-ninety-five? (*Beat.*) You take the bread out of our mouths. It's heartbreaking to say how much we lost on that. And please. I won't even discuss the losses on "Water on Fire, an Oral History of the Children of Hiroshima."

SARAH. Hey. It's just books. You know? I see what's happening here. You'll all use these issues as leverage, whatever the cost. Hey, I know what I'm talking about. Listen, I talk to other actors, and it's so fucking dull. It's just this crushing bore—they're all dying from their dogmas. What they will or will not do, and it's a total snooze. Who cares? It doesn't matter. It just doesn't make a difference.

ISAAC. No, it does matter. It does make a difference. They should care. It matters to them. Otherwise, you end up? What? Heinrich Mann doing little drawings at his desk at Warners. Kazan in a cold sweat, saying yes to anything. All the little failures of spirit—they add up and they add up badly. But, of course, that's the American seduction, isn't it? Not a thing matters here, it's all disposable. Forget your history, forget what you believed in, forget your fire. Forget your fire. (*Pause.*) Leave your fire at the door. You see, Sarah, it matters very much what I choose to fight for. (*Beat.*) So, Aaron. Let me ask you, from a literary standpoint, not a commercial one, why should I publish "Rising Tide"?

AARON. (*Laughs slightly, closes his eyes.*) No. Please. Hey, I'm not that dumb.

SARAH. Well, it's true, honey, you've given, you know, all these terribly mercantile reasons and all, but no literary—

AARON. Yeah, well, don't count on my weakness as a critical thinker, Dad. I'm hip to you. One by one, point by point, I could say, "Oh, the book deals in themes of blah-blah-blah." And you would say, "Oh, no, it doesn't. If that's what you think the book deals in, you're wrong. A book that *does* deal in blah-blah-blah, I would be very interested in publishing. But this book here doesn't, son.

Sorry. Find me a nice German novel about a village in '34 to have translated."

ISAAC. Do me at least the favor of not telling me what I would say to you if you presented an argument to me I haven't heard.

AARON. No. Of course. (*Beat. HE smiles.*) No, I'm not much of a reader, we know. I'm more comfortable, you tell me, with the balance sheet and the projections. The numbers don't lie. All that. (*Pause.*) And all done with a smirk, as if you've always held the opinion that making a lot of money was somehow vulgar. For a publisher. (*Beat.*) I just don't get it. Are your literary opinions so profoundly held that they hold to the point where your children have to halt you? Is this ceaseless drive to run us into the ground circling any particular point, Dad, or is it just that in the six years since Mother died, you've become suicidal? Because you're way too smart to stand on ceremony over Anthony-fucking-Trollope. (*Beat.*) I *think*.

ISAAC. This, Aaron, is simply beneath contempt. This line of reasoning, it's gutter reasoning, kiddo, and—

AARON. Maybe, but ever since your wife died, if we had a graph curve it would look like the north face of Everest from '81 on.

ISAAC. I wouldn't confuse high standards with missing your mother.

AARON. Yeah, well, the thing is, I don't think this has anything to do with "standards." What I think is that you are a man who has lost his sense of humor.

ISAAC. My *what?*

AARON. You've lost your sense of humor. What happened to the low joke? The frivolous gesture?

Bawdiness? You have no time for a laugh. That's why you should publish this book. That's my best argument.

ISAAC. Excuse me, let me get this straight here. I've lost my sense of humor and if I publish the Val Chenard book, I'll get it back? What're you? Nuts?

MARTIN. It's true, Dad, you've become this Cotton Mather type. You're gonna drop dead from rigor any day now. It's true, Sarah, tell him.

SARAH. Hey, I don't know what to say. I see you smirking, Martin, and I hate this. And besides, what do I know about it? I sing songs to eight-year-olds about trichinosis. I shouldn't even be here. But it's true, Daddy, you get more and more intractable, more isolated in your positions.

AARON. You don't go out. You don't see anyone, you sit around with your illustrated letters, your collection of first editions, signed postcards, sneaking off to auctions—

ISAAC. Please, please, this is—

AARON. He bought a postcard of Adolph Hitler's. A little drawing.

ISAAC. Enough.

AARON. Well, what is that *about*?

MARTIN. A postcard of Hitler's?

ISAAC. He painted, you know that, as a boy. I mean, once he was a boy. He sent a postcard on which he had painted a little watercolor of a church. He painted mostly churches. Landmarks in old Vienna. It had a fascination for me. Done in 1916. It wasn't cheap, but it triggered something. I don't know. A view of a world. I am out of step with myself lately, here in New York. I am out of step with myself.

MARTIN. I understand all that, but I don't understand why that precludes publishing Aaron's book. It's a comic novel. A little book. You just can't give everything equal weight, equal moral weight—

ISAAC. Maybe you can. Maybe you should. Maybe that's exactly the problem.

MARTIN. No. I don't think so. For you, rejecting this book becomes this—affirmation—of how you're supposed to live your life, saying "no" to everything. Let me ask you this: You've become a pretty good publisher of books about horror. It's all death camps and napalm and atrocities with you.

ISAAC. Martin—

MARTIN. The question is—just because you've started to deal in historical hardware, do you imagine that makes you above some sort of reproach? It's "Oh, we can't criticize Isaac Geldhart, we've gotta take him dead serious. After all, he published 'Hazlitt on Cannibalism.'" Well, to my mind, all that makes you is a very cautious academic pornographer, a sensationlalist with Sulka ties. "See the bodies pile up, watch the dead, see how bad everything is. Why bother engaging?"

ISAAC. This is rich coming from you who has deliberately shut himself away from all interaction up there in Poughkeepsie. You, with your seed-hybrids. Humorless? No, I don't think so. I am just so afraid of this trash piling up around us. I am afraid of the young. *You.* Let me tell you—I am. "Publish this book 'cause you're not funny anymore." My God, I prefer at least your arguments about fiscal doom, but spare me that playing-to-the-balcony crap about missing your mom. I am destroying this company because life is not worth living without your mother? Let me tell you, that wasn't the greatest marriage in the world. I don't think about her a lot these days. So phooey to that approach—stick to the numbers, Aaron.

SARAH. (*Cuts him off—furious.*) Who do you think you're talking about? That's my mother you're talking about. Please! What the hell is the matter with you? Do you hear yourself? Aaron's trying to help. But all I can see is you treating people badly. Treating Aaron with this superior bullying contempt.

AARON. No, hey, it's what I signed on for. You get used to it. It's like you can insult anyone as long as it's done sort of elegantly.

ISAAC. Who? I do this? I really do this? But think about what you're asking me to do. You want me to change the direction of this company. To do so will drive me mad. I don't even know how to. You've gotta bear with me a little. So what if I'm humorless? Surely that's not a valid reason for taking over my life's work? I would say that a sense of humor is nice, but really, in the end, beside the point.

MARTIN. Maybe. I hope not. When was the last time we had dinner together, Pop?

ISAAC. I always ask, but you turn me down cold, so I don't ask anymore. Don't blame me for that. I made an effort to remain close but—

MARTIN. Yes, sure. On terms that are unlivable. (*HE lights a smoke.*)

ISAAC. I know. I'm tough in a restaurant, but I—what is this *smoking* business? What are you doing *smoking*? You have no business smoking, Martin.

MARTIN. Your obsession over the martini, for instance. Only a miserable man could require such precision in his drink. The little ice container that has to be three-quarters filled to keep the extra martini perfectly cold. The "problem" with the twist. You actually, I sat there— you said to the waiter, "There's a problem with the twist." You actually—I mean, it used to be funny. But grimly gnawing and hacking away at your salmon—sending it back—you sent it back *three times*.

ISAAC. (*With a contemptuous shrug.*) It wasn't right.

MARTIN. Yeah, well, the maitre'd practically stabbed you. I would have applauded. That was the last time we had dinner together.

ISAAC. I thought we had a nice time, Martin.

MARTIN. It was like dinner with Duvalier. Both of them.

AARON. Dad, do you remember when we had a best-seller? It was seven years ago. And it kept us alive. This book can go the same way. Can't you just simply trust me—once. Just now—once.

ISAAC. No. Not on this.

MARTIN. Then I'll sign over my shares of this company to Aaron. He'd be the majority stockholder. I don't want to do that to you, but believe me, I will. Because Mom left us those shares to do what we pleased with. So why push it?

SARAH. Hey, hold on, Martin, what are you doing? Come on, are you kidding here?

ISAAC. Oh, so that's where we are. So how did it go, Aaron? You called up your brother and made him an offer?

That is what you learned at Wharton? Bought you a nice degree, didn't I?

SARAH. Listen, Aaron. This is not just some faceless take-over. Martin. People don't recover. Families, they just fold up, you know? Never to speak again. Are we like that? That sort of family? Over money? You've got to find some way to compromise. All of you. Because this is just horseshit.

ISAAC. I sense your little sister would not be in on your takeover. So, Sarah, darling?

AARON. You cannot possibly win this one, Dad. There's just no way.

SARAH. Hold it. Why don't you bother asking me? I'm not going to sit here like some dumb—nobody bothers asking me what I think. "What does she think?" (*Beat.*) What I think is this. I don't want to turn this into some sort of horrible little ... *thing*. But, Martin, if you hand your stocks to Aaron, then I'll hand mine over to Dad. (*Shrugs, shakes her head.*) Well, sorry. But nobody asks *me*.

AARON. Sarah.

MARTIN. Hey, you know, Sarah, it might not be such a bad idea to let this thing run its course.

SARAH. Why? Because you're enjoying yourself?

ISAAC. So, there you have it. This is, I think, a stalemate.

AARON. Sarah, what are you doing?

ISAAC. Think now, Aaron, didn't Wharton provide you with the next step? (*Silence.*) Why don't you take some time to think it over?

AARON. I have Val in the library. He'll be outta here. He's not just gonna ...

ISAAC. Well, I will ask him to wait. You talk this over without me. My position is clear. I will *not* compromise. I will not be manipulated. But I am not sure that you should either. (*HE exits. Silence in his wake.*)

SARAH. God, he is a tricky bastard.

AARON. Oh, yes.

MARTIN. I need, I think, a drink about now.

AARON. I mean, the idea of you selling your stock to Dad—and, by the way, what's he going to pay you with? Some first editions? Terrific. His collection of illustrated letters? He just went into hock on that Hitler postcard. You want that on your wall?

SARAH. He hung it up?

AARON. Look, there's no cash. We're on empty here.

SARAH. He needs to see a negotiable way out. Bend a little, he'll bend too.

AARON. It's way past that. He got you to offer him your stock. The man'll have fifty-five percent, just what he's after. And if you do that, ultimately, you'll be killing him.

SARAH. But wouldn't taking control from him do him in just as surely—and a hell of a lot more viciously? Have you ever thought that you're acting out of sheer anger towards him? Nothing to do with saving the company? Just rage?

AARON. And if I am? So? What if you're giving into him out of some need to be loved? That's not just as bad?

SARAH. Hey—

AARON. Get ready for next season—"Lullabies from the Warsaw Ghetto." On every remainder shelf in the country.

MARTIN. I'm going to have a drink. This is exhausting. (*HE exits. Silence.*)

SARAH. Why is he smoking and drinking all over the place? What's with him? When did he start? He knows he's supposed to be careful.

AARON. I don't know. I've never been able to read anyone in this family, so don't ask me. (*Beat.*) What do I do now? 'Cause I guess I actually seem to have finally blown it here.

SARAH. I'm sorry, Aaron.

AARON. Well, I just have to find a way to think of this as a positive.

SARAH. Aaron, I'm trying to do the right thing, to do the most right thing.

AARON. No, you're trying to do exactly what I did. You're trying to get his approval. (*Beat.*) I had this idiot notion that he and I'd sit here at this table talking about books. And really he has—not once solicited my opinion, not once asked me what I was reading, over a cup of coffee, which is all I wanted.

SARAH. I know. Listen I'm so dumb I fly across the country because he asks me to. I—look at me—dress like a refugee from "Little Women." I think of important issues to—I actually sat on the plane tearing through back issues of the "New Republic" and "The Nation," trying to find witty things to knock him dead with. And last month, he sent a bunch of S.J. Perlman first editions. Why? No note.

Nothing. But I sit there for hours thinking, "What's he trying to tell me? Be funnier?" I mean, really.

AARON. Last week, someone asked him what you were up to. He told them you were a clown for hire for children's birthday parties. This, after he saw you on the UNICEF anniversary show. Looked at the TV and mumbled, "Americans," as if you were a foreigner.

SARAH. A birthday clown. That's terrific. I love it.

AARON. Yeah, well, he introduced me at the ABA as his bookkeeper, so you're not alone. (*Beat.*) Look. Seeing as this is pretty much over, we should, at least, be able to have a meal together. Brooklyn. "Garjulos"? The puttanesca is still like blood.

SARAH. Oh, shit, Aaron, I can't. Really. I have to catch the nine o'clock to the coast. We're doing "K" tomorrow.

AARON. "K"?

SARAH. The letter "K," yeah. It's my letter.

AARON. Oh. May I ask you this? Are you still involved with your producer? Is that still on?

SARAH. Why? I mean?

AARON. I'm just curious. It was an issue for you last time I saw you. "This older man." That's still happening?

SARAH. "Happening" implies action, you know? Motion. I just sit around waiting for the guy, repeating lines to myself that would send a sane person running a million miles. Like, "Oh, he's leaving his wife of fifteen years. It was over anyway." So mostly, I wait. (*Beat.*) And yes, fine, he goes days without calling.

AARON. But you settle for that? An older man pushing you, doling out little bits here and there—?

SARAH. No, I admit it, you don't have to press the goddamn point. He's absolutely the cliché of a father fixation.

AARON. Well, just last week, our father accused me of being a person most free within a cliché. He said I was liberated by banality, so. That is that?

SARAH. What're you going to do?

AARON. What can I do? I'm gonna back down, and help steer us through bankruptcy. It's okay—This thing was doomed from the beginning, from the start. I went out with Chenard in college.

SARAH. With? Oh, my God, Aaron, honey. Is that why the book has been so—

AARON. No, I don't think so. I mean, the book is good. This is not a clouded issue.

SARAH. I didn't know, Aaron. I knew that you were ... but I mean, I just didn't know. You've been so silent.

AARON. No, well, yes. It was a thing. We used to have things. Everybody had a little "thing." Judy doesn't know. Nobody. He liked me because I admitted I knew nothing about literature, only about maybe making a profit in the service of art. He thought I was actually totally naive. Which, of course, I was. (*Beat.*) We have dinner. The people we went to school with are off, you know, doing bad performance art in Hoboken, or in closed sessions with the SEC over insider jobs downtown. Nothing in between. I'm in publishing. We have this link.

SARAH. So this has been with you?

AARON. And I am almost totally domesticated. Judy bought me these slippers from Brooks Brothers. With lamb's wool. I looked at them and thought, "Shackles, goddammit. How do I end up here?"

SARAH. I am sorry, Aaron. That's hard. That's so hard.

AARON. No. It was pathetic to have thought of this as my big chance. To prove to Dad—I mean, I must think like a seven-year-old.

SARAH. Well, I'm still a toddler, so at least you're ahead of me.

AARON. Too bad we couldn't have a bite.

SARAH. Yeah, well, I've gotta get back. I have the letter "K" to take care of. Such as it is.

AARON. And a father fixation to nurture, right?

MARTIN. (*Enters with a drink in hand.*) Dad is sitting in the library with your writer, Aaron.

AARON. What's he doing?

MARTIN. His Decline of the West, part three speech. Chenard is laughing.

AARON. Look, Sarah, if you were to back me, the very worst is that Dad will have been wrong. Well, he should be able to learn to live with that. It's not the end of the world. He'll simply have been mistaken, and I'll have helped him—we'll have helped him. Come on.

SARAH. Look, maybe we should all just pull back. When he comes in, we'll try and start this from scratch. Just reason it out, okay?

MARTIN. I'm not pulling back. Hey, it's Aaron's. I'm out, and I don't give a fuck what you publish really.

SARAH. Hey, come on Martin. Please. What are you talking about?

MARTIN. We go months without speaking to one another. We're all afraid of each other—slightly put off. There's some sort of competitiveness under the surface, and I've never cared for it. We're better off keeping away from each other. And more than that, let me tell you—I am above this struggle.

ISAAC. (*Entering.*) So, its getting late. We all have places to go, and I'm tired. How do you want to handle this?

MARTIN. Publish *Hustler* or publish Proust. I don't want to have anything to do with it anymore. Your books. God. I am so tired of these books. And your endless posturing, position-taking, ranting, judging. The only thing I miss is Mom. She wouldn't put up with any of this crap for a second. She'd know what to do. Damn it. I just—coming down here is too much. It's done me in. I miss Mom.

ISAAC. The only part I believe is the last. Such poison. Why such poison, Martin? Always?

MARTIN. Poison! You want to talk about poison? Look at what you've done. You've created a family of literary zombies. You know that people are afraid of you. It's why you've gotten so far. Yes. "Isaac Geldhart knows something, he came from some awful childhood in Europe that nobody knows about." He has a "seer-like standing in the book world." Blah-Blah-Blah—phooey. Let me tell you, we're fucked up by it. I grew up running around this building. When I was eight, you gave me the Iliad in Greek so that someday I could read it. Monster! People's lives are ruined by books and they're all you know how to relate to, Dad. You too, Aaron, for all your talk. You too, Sarah,

pretending you hate to read. Sometimes I want to take a
pruning shears and do an Oedipus on myself. I counted my
books last week. Do you know how many I have? Want to
take a guess? (*No one says anything.*) Fourteen thousand,
three hundred, and eighty-six. The sixty crates of books
that Mom left me. Well, I finally had them carted up the
Hudson, but I had to have shelves built. The whole house.
Every room. And instead of just guessing—I was, I
mean—speechless. A wreck of a life. It just flashed before
my eyes. No sex, no people, just books 'til I die. Dickens.
In *French*. The bastard didn't write in French. What the
fuck am I doing with "Dombey and Son" in French? The
twelve-volume "Conquest of Mexico." Two hundred
cookbooks. The "Oxford World Classics," the little ones
with the blue bindings, you know?
    ISAAC. You got that?
    MARTIN. They're all just words. And this is life, and
besides, I hear the book chains are now selling pre-emptive
strike video games, so why bother anyway? I'm out.
    ISAAC. But really, there are limits, sweetheart.
    MARTIN. Yes. That's exactly right. There are limits. I
believe I know that. Hey, I spent most of my sixteenth
year getting chemotherapy, remember? And it's not that
long ago, I can still feel it. I cannot waste my life. I feel
you people dragging me into this thing. You want this
confrontation, Dad. You want nothing more than your
children gathered around you, fighting. Well forget it. You
don't know what I feel in my back, in my bones. I wake
up some days and I'm crying. I think I'm still at Sloan-
Kettering, lying there hairless and white and filling up with
glucose from a drip. Hey! I can't get that time back. I feel

all the needles, some days, my lymph nodes, and I'm sweating. And part of my life is spent in fear, waiting. I know none of us has forever, know that very well, and I care very much how I spend my time. And involved in an internecine war over a publishing house, is, by my reckoning, Father, a dead waste. *And* if I choose to live with plants as an assistant lecturer at an over-rated seven-sisters school, *that* is my goddamn choice. But let's clear us something finally: I am not a goddamn gardener, and you are never going to goad me back into this life by calling me one. And Sarah is not a clown at children's birthday parties, Dad, and Aaron isn't a fucking accountant. You are really charming about your superiority, Dad. But you're really alone, too. This Nazi book jag of yours—it scares me.

ISAAC. I spent a couple of days, a little boy, wandering around after the liberation. I saw a particular kind of man—a wraith-like figure—who could only have been in the camps. But with a brown pinstripe suit, a fleur-de-lis on his tie and manicured nails, trying to pick up where he left off, as if you could. I never say anything about this. Why talk? Why bother? I wasn't in the camps. You know? They're busy throwing the Farbers and the Hirsches into the ovens, and I'm happily eating smoked eels in the basement, with my Stendahl and Dumas. What did I know? I was protected, sheltered by my cousins. And then I got out of the basement and into the wrecked world. I came to this country. You re-invent yourself. Make it as a bon-vivant in Manhattan. Meet this woman—this extraordinary woman. Marry. Have these kids. Go to so many cocktail parties, host so many more ... and they ...

haunt. (*Beat.*) I have kept my eyes closed to the world outside the basement for so long. The wrecked world all around us. But I can no longer close my eyes. (*HE turns to Aaron.*) My son. You are fired. I will give you a week to clear your desk, and I will give you letters of recommendation. But I will not speak to you, I will not communicate with you, I will not ... (*Pause.*) ... *give at all.* Kiddo. To the victor go the spoils.

SARAH. Wait a second, wait a second. I see what you're doing. You want to use *me* to screw Aaron. And you think I would go along with that? You think that's the kind of person I am? That I'd just sit still and watch you? Why—because I feel sorry for you because you weren't in a camp?

ISAAC. Sarah—

SARAH. No. I am going to hand my shares to Aaron. Because you just don't understand. You don't know how to love.

AARON. Wait a second. Let's be clear about this. You just handed me control of this company.

SARAH. Yes. I did.

AARON. You did this to yourself. It didn't have to happen.

ISAAC. Do what you must.

AARON. (*Quietly furious.*) I warned you. I explained it to you. But you ignore all the signs. You just proceed self-destructively, asking for help, asking to be usurped, up-ended, damn it. Do you want to hate me? (*Beat.*) Well, go ahead. Hate me. But we need cash. I have had an offer. Japanese. And you will no longer run the company, you will be kicked onto the board. I have tried to warn you. But with Martin and Sarah's stock—with control in my hands, I have no choice. We will be backed by some men in Tokyo who won't give a fuck whether I publish Val Chenard or Racing Forum so long as it turns a buck in their direction. And you knew this was coming. You knew it could only end up like this. Well, at least you'll be taken care of. You won't starve to death. I'm sorry. I simply have no choice.

ISAAC. You understand, Aaron, sweetheart. You will just be part of the big pile, the big carcinogenic pile of trash, building up all around you, as life itself no longer seems real.

AARON. Yeah, well, you know, that's not my problem. That's *your* problem, Dad. It's not my fault that life does seem real to me, and I can make peace with that. I don't have a holocaust to pin on my chest. I have my family. My city. Some continuity. The way I think. My friends. I don't want to set life back to its beginnings, and I'm not burdened by thinking I'm one of the world's great thinkers, either. All I can do with the "carcinogenic pile of trash" is sift through it. That's all anyone can do. But my life does seem totally real to me. I do not need to suffer in order to feel alive, Pop. I'm sorry. I'm going to have dinner with my author.

ISAAC. (*As AARON starts out.*) Aaron. I hope it works out for you.

(AARON exits. ISAAC crosses to the window, looks out.)

ISAAC. This city. When I got off the boat, I said, "It's going to be so good now, this life, it's all going to be so full." It was snowing.

SARAH. I'm sorry. I have a plane to catch. Daddy ... (*SHE exits.*)

MARTIN. Dad, why don't we get some dinner? We could take the car. It never gets used. Go across the bridge.

ISAAC. That is not possible.

(The LIGHTS fade.)

ACT II

*Three and a half years later. An old apartment in Gramercy
Park. ISAAC is sitting in a chair, staring out the
window. A fierce winter SNOWSTORM swirls around
and down over the park. The RADIO plays, and the
RADIATOR hisses steam, gurgles, protests, coughs.
The apartment is not so much a home as it is an
archive. Floor to ceiling—the room is dominated by
books. Though there are also gaping holes, gaps on the
shelves where volumes are missing. There are also
framed letters—all of which are embellished with
drawings. ISAAC has a frayed, fogged-in air about him.
The door BUZZER rings. ISAAC sighs, turns off the
RADIO. HE puts on his tie and shoes, and is getting on
his jacket as MARTIN enters—layered in snow, parka,
scarf, gloves, and boots. HE stands for a moment,
catching his breath.*

MARTIN. (*Putting his coat, etc., on a hook in the
hall.*) Didn't you hear the buzzer?
ISAAC. (*Eager.*) You want tea? Is it cold? It looks a
little cold outside?
MARTIN. I had to stand there, struggling with these
keys in the ice and the ... (*Pause. HE sighs.*) How are you?
ISAAC. (*Shrugs.*) Who the hell knows, you know? I
didn't think you'd get in. I hear on WNYC the trains are
backed up to Lake Placid.

39

MARTIN. No, I came in last night, I—
ISAAC. I see. I see. I see. Last night. You ...?
MARTIN. Stayed at a friend's.

(ISAAC nods, not thrilled.)

MARTIN. You ate?
ISAAC. (*Not interested.*) Maybe with the snow, the girl
won't come.
MARTIN. The cleaning girl?
ISAAC. This place is—who can live this way? (*Yells
suddenly.*) Goddamn it! Who? The kitchen is—have you
ever tried to steam a squash? I stand there. It's a room full
of yellow pulp.
MARTIN. (*Smiles.*) Please.
ISAAC. (*Resigned.*) Martin, I'm telling you, you can't
run a place this big with only a woman who comes in once
a week from Belize. The dust, it's like a nuclear winter in
this place. I'm—(*ISAAC runs out of steam.*) You have to
take three showers a day.
MARTIN. Dad. The social worker. That's today. You
remember?
ISAAC. No, no, no. What do you think, I'm an idiot?
Today is the maid and Thursday is the Sotheby lady.
MARTIN. (*Quiet.*) It's the psychiatric social worker.
You agreed. I came into town because you asked me—
ISAAC. (*Yelling.*) Do I look to you like a man who
hasn't got a calendar? Thursday is the social worker. Today
is Tuesday, the cleaning lady! Please!
MARTIN. Today, actually, Isaac, *is,* in point of fact,
Thursday.

(There is silence.)

ISAAC. Without Miss Barzakian how'm I supposed to know my appointments? Idiotic. To have even consented to this.

MARTIN. It would help if you could remember the days of the week.

ISAAC. What for? Just a slab of days, this. What do you do? You go back to Aaron? With reports?

MARTIN. Yes. He asks.

ISAAC. He asks? And you tell him, "He's doddering, he's slobbering, he's mortifying, the kitchen is a horror? He can't tie his shoes." That sort of thing? Because frankly, if that's the case, I'm better off—

MARTIN. *(Suddenly suspicious.)* What do you mean the "Sotheby Lady"—what were you talking about before?

ISAAC. I didn't say anything, I didn't say—

MARTIN. What did you do? Have you been trying to get rid of more stuff?

ISAAC. Musselblat the attorney tells me if I can raise enough, I should be able to make a reasonable offer to get back the company, so—

MARTIN. *(Disgusted and exhausted.)* Oh, Jesus, Dad. Isaac. What's the matter with you?

ISAAC. I've gotta try, don't I?

MARTIN. We're in chapter 11. What do you think you can do? It would take a superhuman effort, and you're not in any shape ...

ISAAC. What do you know about business? What have you ever known about business? Please. Please. *(ISAAC takes a moment.*) You know, yesterday, I saw the most magnificent pair of shoes on Irving Place on a young guy, and he had to have someone makin' 'em, I tell ya, 'cause there ain't no guy in this hell hole of a town who can do that particular suede—in one *piece*—I tell you. Probably he was English, and I followed him. I'd buy 'em, even if they were the wrong size. You get a guy to copy 'em, there you are. (*HE looks bitterly at his son.*) I'll tell you something. I can waste my day in so many goddamn ways, I tell you.

(THEY both just sit for a moment.)

MARTIN. Dad, have you been for a walk? The park is white. Maybe if it stops snowing.

ISAAC. Do we have to talk? To sit here talking with you—it's like talking to strangers. I really, these little trips in from the country of yours. I don't need 'em, I really don't. I can handle the Sotheby people just fine.

MARTIN. It's the social worker, and it wasn't my idea.

ISAAC. (*Scornful.*) No, of course not. But if Aaron says I'm incompetent, there's gotta be something to it, right? After all, he sure did such a good job with the company, didn't he?

MARTIN. Nobody is saying anything about your being incompetent—

ISAAC. (*Explodes.*) Please! Remember who you're talking to! The impertinence! (*ISAAC crosses away from Martin.*)

MARTIN. (*Looks at a pile of bills.*) But why didn't you pay the phone people? It's past due. Can't you see this only serves to substantiate—

ISAAC. It's a maelstrom of papers. Who can keep track of them all? Maybe if they were at least in different colors. (*HE sees MARTIN looking at some empty book shelves.*) I have to sell it all. Besides, the disability is up any day now. That's a big check every month to do without. What am I supposed to do?

MARTIN. You sold the old Everyman Encyclopedias?

ISAAC. I got nothing for it. You know what I did? I had to go see those pricks at Gotham. I had to walk in the door like some kind of huckster, like it's a grapefruit. I wish your brother'd seen it. (*HE looks at Martin.*) Tell me something, why do you dress like you're some sort of Paul Bunyan character? It's unbecoming.

MARTIN. I'm sorry. I'll wear a suit next time.

(Silence.)

ISAAC. What do you hear from your sister?

MARTIN. That you still hang up the phone on her.

ISAAC. I'd like to get the hell out of this town. A building blew up just across the park. Apparently there was a cloud of asbestos and now there's cancer for everyone. A janitor was parboiled. The whole street was a freak show.

MARTIN. No, I know. We've talked about this.

ISAAC. Of course, the management company on this property, I think I last saw them in '59, when we signed the papers, and—

(There is a BUZZ. MARTIN crosses to the hall for the intercom.)

MARTIN. (*Into intercom.*) Hello?

ISAAC. They can't hear you. It doesn't work. You can only buzz, not talk, so if, per chance, it happens to be a mugger, well, you're fine.

MARTIN. (*Into intercom.*) Hello?

MARGE HACKETT. (*Over intercom.*) It's Marge Hackett.

ISAAC. Occasionally, it works.

MARTIN. Come up to three. (*MARTIN pushes the button.*) Dad, Can I give you some advice?

(*ISAAC says nothing.*)

MARTIN. Just try and answer yes or no. You don't have to—you don't have to do the Isaac Geldhart show. It's not required. They don't let you off on charm. They don't even get it, these people, and if you—

ISAAC. No, I get it. Quit your carping, would you? Making me ill. (*HE turns his back to Martin.*) Standing here giving instructions like I'm your photosynthesis class or something.

(*A KNOCK is heard.*)

MARTIN. Dad, she's here.

(*ISAAC exits.*
MARGE HACKETT enters. A woman in her fifties—maybe, hard to be sure.)

MARTIN. Hi. We talked on the phone, we spoke. Martin Geldhart.

MARGE. Oh, yes, right. Sure.

MARTIN. I didn't know if you'd make it here.

MARGE. The snow doesn't bother me. I don't mind it.

MARTIN. (*Shakes his head, looks at her.*) Listen. I know you came all the way here, but I don't think this is the greatest time.

MARGE. On the phone, you said there are bad days.

MARTIN. I would say this appears to be one of them.

MARGE. The depression? It's also, the weather doesn't help much. It can do people in.

MARTIN. Maybe you should come back.

MARGE. Well, I'm here. And your brother...?

MARTIN. Aaron?

MARGE. Was very insistent. Look. The Department is swamped. To get these appointments, and then to get someone to come to the house, it's tough. Why drag it on?

MARTIN. (*Resigned.*) Okay. (*Beat.*) He yells. He was always a bit of a yeller, but now—

MARGE. I am used to it. I don't—it doesn't scare me. But I have to call in. Is there a phone anywhere I can use?

MARTIN. The kitchen. (*HE points.*) Miss Hackett, I just want you to know—I think this whole business is a big mistake.

(*ISAAC enters.*)

MARGE. Noted. (*SHE exits.*)

MARTIN. She's calling her office. I'll leave you alone.

(ISAAC says nothing.)

MARTIN. Please don't stand here yelling at her. Would you? Don't do a number on her. *(Pause. No response.)* When she comes in, I'm going to leave you alone.

ISAAC. What? You think I need you to sit here in the room with me?

(MARTIN nods, starts to exit.)

ISAAC. Martin, how's my tie?

(MARGE enters.)

MARTIN. *(Adjusting Isaac's tie.)* It's fine. *(Exits.)*

MARGE. Your phone, it doesn't seem to be working, it's out.

ISAAC. The weather. But you found it?

MARGE. I did find it.

ISAAC. Because sometimes I misplace it. You see, it doesn't ring. *(Beat.)* Isaac Geldhart.

MARGE. Yes. Marge Hackett.

ISAAC. Listen to that. "It doesn't ring." Already that sounds like special pleading.

MARGE. Not necessarily.

ISAAC. Actually, to tell you the truth, what it is, is a *relief*. I spent so many years waiting for phones to ring, sitting about, so now ...

MARGE. The silence is welcome. I understand.

ISAAC. Do we know each other? You look ... no. Tell me, did the woman offer you a coffee?

MARGE. I didn't see anyone.

ISAAC. It's Tuesday.

MARGE. No. It's not Tuesday.

ISAAC. No, it's *Thursday.* She has a tendency not to show. Also, she ain't listed, so I'm fucked. (*Pause.*) Forgive me. I'm trying to be competent. That's the thing you need to know, is it not?

MARGE. Mr. Geldhart, nothing is being determined here.

ISAAC. Oh, forgive me, I was under the impression that something *was* being determined.

MARGE. No. This is a process. No one person can make a dispensation, come to a conclusion.

ISAAC. No one person? There's more of you to come? A tribunal?

MARGE. It's not that bad.

ISAAC. (*Looks at the disarray around.*) There is a mess. You should watch out, because there was asbestos across the park. I'm sure it drifted over. I try not to breathe, which is a hell of a trick. So.

MARGE. So. You understand, then, why I came here, what it is I'm doing here? I repeat—nothing is being determined by just one visit and—

ISAAC. (*Suddenly furious.*) They send a woman into my house to see if I'm a whacko, and nothing is being determined here? The—the—the paperwork that has come flying into this apartment from all the—

MARGE. Please, Mr. Geldhart, you have to, you don't have to—

ISAAC. Why the hell don't you just tell me exactly what I have to do?

MARTIN. (*In the doorway.*) Dad.

ISAAC. Oh, for God's sake, Martin, they sent over here a—look at this woman.

MARGE. (*To Martin.*) It's okay. Why don't you just leave us for a bit, see how it goes?

ISAAC. Maybe both of you should please just leave me alone. Do you think anyone wants to be seen like this? I mean, it's so fucking vulgar ...

MARGE. (*To Martin.*) It's all right.

(MARTIN looks at Isaac, exits.)

MARGE. We usually do this at the office. It took a bending of the rules to even get the department to think about letting someone come to the house.

ISAAC. I see. Well.

MARGE. Your son, Aaron, he wanted it not to be a nightmare for you.

ISAAC. How thoughtful, such a thoughtful boy, always has been.

MARGE. Our offices aren't so great. He saw that. He was very protective, and he's quite persuasive. So. Here I am.

ISAAC. Yes, you can imagine how grateful I am that I don't have to go to the Cloisters to see a shrink.

MARGE. Actually, we're not in the Cloisters. We're just around the corner, so to speak, across from Bellevue. (*Beat.*) Your son said you might be a little cranky.

ISAAC. A little cranky? Fuck him. That's Aaron's brilliant analysis of my situation, "a little bit cranky"?

MARGE. No, that was Martin. Aaron wasn't so mild.

ISAAC. Aaron. Do you know when last I saw him? Three and a half years ago! Three and a half years. Years!

MARGE. Do you know why I'm here, though? Aside from—

ISAAC. (*Cuts her off, savage.*) I don't give a shit. Three and a half years, I said, and every day I don't see him is a victory. And as for this one, a couple of times a year only, and only because he's weaker than the other two, and I'm not *that* hard. "A little cranky." Fuck them! You got any children, Miss Hackett?

MARGE. Yes, I have children, yeah. I do have children, and—

ISAAC. And do your children think you're crazy?

MARGE. Yes.

ISAAC. Do they really? Well then, Bob's your aunt, as the Brits like to say. So, how are things at Sotheby's?

MARGE. Sotheby?

ISAAC. What do you think of the collection?

MARGE. Pardon me? What are you talking about?

ISAAC. (*Pointing to some framed letters on the wall.*) The illustrated letters, those. Believe me, I've seen you eyeing 'em. You'll see, just like I said on the phone, the collection—I have one piece that's exquisitely ironic.

MARGE. I'm not from Sotheby. I'm from Social Services.

ISAAC. (*Letting that one go.*) I have here something that's not up on the walls ... There was a filing system when—I used to have Miss Barzakian rummaging around in here doing alphabetical orders and such. The perfect job for a person who was never married. She had an Eastern European's passion for chaos. (*ISAAC takes a moment.*)

Of course, what she is now is dead, of course. You know? And we had a link, let me tell you.

MARGE. What was that? (*Beat.*) Mr. Geldhart?

ISAAC. We were both refugees. New York, for some of us, for many, who got out of "that kind of Europe"—how do you explain such a link? We didn't come as husks. We came with some decent socks and some hand-made shoes. Our Europe. (*HE stops, looks at her.*) But you are not interested in this, forgive me.

MARGE. No, it's interesting.

ISAAC. (*Overriding her with a small, sad smile.*) No, of course you're not. You came to look at the collection. Forgive me. My mind wanders, so they tell me.

MARGE. Are you toying with me, Mr. Geldhart?

ISAAC. I'm not toying with anyone, Miss Hackett, not at all.

MARGE. Do you mind if I smoke?

ISAAC. Nobody smokes anymore.

MARGE. Well, I do.

ISAAC. Yeah, me too. Must be nuts, eh? I'll join you.

MARGE. At the hospital, they don't permit it. Which seems a kind of one-upsmanship to me. Frankly, you know. Bash the smokers. Lord over 'em. Give it to 'em. And there are all these signs on the wall. Well, it's a hospital, so you can't complain. But they give you these looks. That's even if you step outside. They have this little quadrangle, and they won't even put a *bench* there.

ISAAC. (*HE lights her cigarette.*) Uh huh? Yes, is that so? That's very interesting, uh ...

MARGE. And they give you these little breaks. It's all highly regulated. But the very worst of it is, the worst is—

there are these women. These insufferable women in white nurses outfits—not even real R.N.s—just volunteers who come in on the Long Island Railroad from *Merrick*. And they create these little *dramas*. My smoking. That constitutes a drama, so I guess life's lost its luster for them, huh? You should see 'em. They have their own refrigerator, and they put labels on cans of Tab. "Do not touch—Molly's Tab." "Debbie's Tuna." And you're forced into the position of acquiescing to them.

ISAAC. Excuse me, I'm sorry, but, do I make you nervous or something?

MARGE. Yes. Why?

ISAAC. I know your type. Divorced. New York State College at New Paltz. Tried to be "with it."

MARGE. If it makes you comfortable to create a little scenario for me, fine. Understand that your son Aaron has suggested competency proceedings be—

ISAAC. Please!

MARGE. Because you have demonstrated a credible inability to manage your own affairs.

ISAAC. And what makes you think you could do such a job? Do you have a formal means of determining levels of responsibility? Rational adult behavior? What? Does the Mayor and Cardinal what's-his-name get together? What? The Skinner people, the Sullivan people? Dewey-Decimal? At least in the *library* world ... (*ISAAC halts.*) No. I can't take this seriously. No.

MARGE. No. Well, neither does your son Martin.

ISAAC. Ah, the Neville Chamberlain of sons.

MARGE. Well, the fact is, we were called upon. It is to be taken seriously.

ISAAC. Did the woman give you a coffee?

MARGE. And you agreed. You said, "Yes." An evaluation was acceptable to you if it would result in your being left alone. Nobody wants to come into somebody's life and—

ISAAC. You are speaking to me as if I were someone to whom logic was a worthwhile approach. If I am ga-ga, logic means nothing, right?

MARGE. Well, I'm new. Maybe with a little experience, I'll begin treating people badly. Look, I really, all I have to do is ask you some questions. (*SHE stares at Isaac.*) We can get it over with. And—it's not as if what I say can determine your fate. If that's what you're afraid of...

ISAAC. What a relief. Okay, shoot.

MARGE. What country, state, city are we in right now?

ISAAC. Are you kidding me? What kind of question is that?

MARGE. It's a perfectly reasonable question.

ISAAC. Next.

MARGE. What month is it?

ISAAC. July, can't you tell?

MARGE. Mr. Geldhart, look

ISAAC. Okay. There is a book company. It has my name on it. And some forty percent of it still belongs to me. Some Japanese own the rest, along with Aaron, who has helped them grind it down into a kind of bankrupt dust. (*Beat.*) So, you see, I've been trying to put together a package. I still know a little money in this town and at the same time, my son, also wouldn't mind eighty-sixing the nips, and he thought if he could get me out of the picture, maybe he could use my forty as leverage. This is what we've got here.

MARGE. You're saying your son is doing all this just to get your stock?

ISAAC. Yes, so. You are a dupe, sweetie. Now, I've got coffee cake, linzer torte and sacher torte. You want some?

(NOBODY says anything for a moment.)

MARGE. Aaron tells me you spent $43,000 on hand-cut suits. What made you think you needed them?

ISAAC. I thought it was going to be a busy year.

MARGE. He says you hardly ever leave this apartment. Is that true?

ISAAC. It was *not* a busy year.

MARGE. And that you've cast off all your friends, you've disengaged.

ISAAC. What? I need to have friends?

MARGE. And the credit card bills?

ISAAC. Staggering! Guilty.

MARGE. You're living on—I mean—I don't understand. What did you think would happen to you when it was all gone?

ISAAC. *(With exaggerated good cheer.)* Who cares?

MARGE. You were diagnosed last year as chronically depressed. You've been on Ellavill three times a day.

ISAAC. I stopped taking it. I could not read. *That* I will not accept! *(Suddenly bright.)* Let me show you the collection. Enough of this, right? You said on the phone that you are a fan of Herzen? Well, I have the first English edition of "Childhood, Youth & Exile." London. 1921. (*HE hands her the Herzen.*) How many can there be of that? A private printing of "Pilgrim's Progress," 1898. All this shelf, Private Press stuff—Coleridge was here, sold it to Bertie Rota in London. Wordsworth here. (*HE picks up a catalogue.*) See? The Geldhart Collection. Look at the prices. That's what you get in London where there's still a market, but here ... Jack London, and Conrad here. And of course, I still got the "Illustrated Letters." I only sold a couple, to make the Visa people happy. They were getting shrill. (*HE sits next to her on the sofa, with the Illustrated Letters file on the coffee table.*)

MARGE. And this is what you love? Books.

ISAAC. Yes. Funny.

MARGE. What? What is it? Did I say something? I—

(*SHE smiles. HE is amused.*)

ISAAC. No, you had this marvelous tone. This anti-intellectual tone one comes across. So. You hate books.

MARGE. Not at all. (*SHE smiles at her little pun.*)

ISAAC. (*Opening the folder.*) There was a time when people used to revel in words. In stories. A kind of perfection, in the air about you, at all times. And people, of course, they used to write. To each other. And how marvelous to accompany the letter with a drawing. A gesture of love—(*Pause.*) Thackeray. Look at it. He bombarded friends with letters. Look at the sketches. He used to illustrate his own novels!

MARGE. It's lovely.

ISAAC. Max Beerbohm. Look at this. George Grosz. Here is, from Max Beckmann, a little note, a sketch. (They chased him out, he ended up dead in the States. A teacher.)

MARGE. Oh!

ISAAC. Osip Mandlestam to his wife. Isaac Babel to his. Orwell from Spain. You begin to see such a blood-thirsty century ... but aren't they all? Maybe. Maybe, I don't know. (*HE looks at her sharply.*) Mind you—it's understood from the get-go, you take the entire collection. I can't bear to think of it's being split up, divvied up all over town—it's to be sold as a piece or nothing, got it?!

MARGE. (*After a moment.*) It's a lovely collection.

ISAAC. You like it?

MARGE. Very much.

ISAAC. (*Clear and quiet and bitter.*) Yeah? Well, me too.

MARGE. I'm sorry.

ISAAC. What?

MARGE. Listen, Mr. Geldhart. I'm going to have someone else do this.

ISAAC. What?

MARGE. I'm sorry. Someone will call from my office. I'm not the one to do this. I hate this. I can't do this.

ISAAC. What? Please, what did I say? Look at the rest of the work, would you?

MARGE. (*Rushing to leave.*) I'm not from Sotheby, and I shouldn't be here. Goodbye, Mr. Geldhart.

ISAAC. I have a letter from Adolph Hitler ...

(*MARGE stops walking.*)

ISAAC. A postcard actually on which he painted a little water-color of a burnt-out church. Bought his art supplies from a Jew. Who thought he had talent. And gave him, just gave him his materials. I mean, I think about that, and what came after ... It's the most crucial part of my collection.

(ISAAC shows the card to MARGE.)

ISAAC. He was not without a certain basic, rudimentary talent, was he not? You would certainly hope that he had been utterly devoid of talent. I mean, it would at least shed some tiny glimmer of light on the subsequent years, on all that came after. But no—it's no slur of muddy-non-color, this. There is something here, yes?

MARGE. I suppose.

ISAAC. It's never actually been appraised, which is why I called your firm.

MARGE. Do you really think I'm from an auction house, Mr. Geldhart?

ISAAC. *(After a moment.)* I have problems.

MARGE. Yes.

ISAAC. Oh, I know I'm getting it wrong a lot of the time. I used to think it was the fog from the pills they gave me, but when I stopped taking the pills ... the fog will not lift. But to simply stand about, helpless. That is not acceptable to me. I am not used to it. I find my dream life so much more interesting, given my current waking one. *(Beat.)* It's getting dark. So early. Every year a little earlier. Have you ever been out into this park?

MARGE. A few times. When my husband was alive.

ISAAC. Oh. I see. Oh. (*Beat.*) Sorry.

MARGE. We had friends who lived across the park. They used to promenade us there, yeah. Fine, it's a nice park, but, the idea of a key bugs me. It's just a *park,* for God's sake.

ISAAC. Capitalism at its worst?

MARGE. Just small-minded. I wasn't looking at the politics of the thing. (*SHE moves towards the door, to leave.*)

ISAAC. I've always hated this park. You need a key to get in it. And there's never anyone there.

MARGE. I was here once before.

ISAAC. What? What was that?

MARGE. 1974. During the crisis. The city crisis, when New York was broke, I was here, in this apartment.

ISAAC. You were in my house before? In this apartment?

MARGE. At work, there are these gruesome meetings, at which they assign all the cases. And I recognized your name.

ISAAC. So we *have* met before?

MARGE. You must have had a lot going on in those days. Yes. And I recognized your name from the case-load, and I didn't say anything. This room is the same. It's not as clean, it's not what it was, but the same.

ISAAC. Forgive me, but I'm lost, I knew I recognized you, but I can't place it, and anyhow, most often, when I think I know someone, I'm wrong. You were here before?

MARGE. There was a reading. Some essayist you published, it was a fundraiser for the library. Because the books were literally rotting, and nobody worked there, and there—

ISAAC. They didn't have a single copy of Joyce's *Exiles.* I went in and exploded.

MARGE. So it *was* a fundraiser.

ISAAC. It was horrible.

MARGE. My husband liked those kinds of things. Mainly for the food. I remember one thing in particular. You didn't have rumaki, which was standard fare for those things, and for that little bit, I was grateful.

(ISAAC pours a drink, offers it to Marge. SHE refuses.)

ISAAC. It *was* a reading. Clayton Broomer, prick of a guy from the *New Yorker*—wrote about architecture. I couldn't stand him, but my wife made me publish his books. He shrilled at everyone in 'em, about how the city got so ugly. Boy, did I hate those things.

MARGE. Me too.

ISAAC. So. Different time, this, eh? Different time.

MARGE. (*Tentative.*) And we talked.

ISAAC. We talked?

MARGE. We stood in the kitchen. And you were intensely annoyed with your wife.

ISAAC. She had a touch of the flag-waver about her.

MARGE. (*Remembering.*) We stood in your kitchen, you and I, drinking vodka and smoking. I remember hearing my husband laughing and making some sort of deal in this room. We'd just watched him rip off a whole plate of Gravad lox from the waitress, and devour it. You were very insulting. You said he had a voice like something from an animal act on public television. I might have been hurt but we were enjoying the vodka ...

ISAAC. Your husband. Tell me, who is this? You sound ...?

MARGE. Bitter? Yeah, well ... *(Pause.)* My husband was Adrian Harrold.

ISAAC. *(Nods, getting it.)* Oh, I see. Jesus Christ. And now you work for social services, shlepping around town with a little briefcase? Adrian Harrold. I remember your husband. The Manhattan Borough President. And in the end, made off with a couple of million, didn't he?

MARGE. The last editorial in the *Times* said, "Drinking from the public trough like a maddened pig ..."

ISAAC. Please, I really, this is not. I did not ...

MARGE. Do you know how they found him? My husband? On the road to Montauk. Actually, at the end of the road. God knows what he was doing. In February out there, by the lighthouse. He had a Biedermeier table in the back of his Lincoln. His wrists and ankles slashed and a bottle of pills on the floor. And then, for weeks afterwards, the funny part, these women would show up with outrageous claims. *(Beat.)* Good for a laugh, at least.

ISAAC. I'm sorry. I am.

MARGE. My husband lied from morning 'til night, and they knew everything. The Mayor. All of them. The only one, really, who knew nothing was, in fact, me.

ISAAC. So, your husband, he left you, what? Nothing?

MARGE. No. He left nothing. I mean, he had his hands in the till. And to me, this is funny—he never shared. It was all for him. *(SHE looks at him.)* I expected to find a drooler. I thought I'd come over here and find a drooler who had had it easy in the old days.

ISAAC. No, unfortunately, I'm not a drooler. So, you came not for an "evaluation," you came 'cause you were curious.

MARGE. Yes.

ISAAC. You came to gloat. You came to see a "drooler."

MARGE. (*Ashamed, perhaps.*) Maybe.

ISAAC. But this is pathetic. It's like nostalgia for a car wreck. So, terrific, you're just another hustler with an agenda.

MARGE. You could say that.

ISAAC. So, what it is is you get a kick out of seeing someone from the old days? And maybe even taking him down? That's a lot of power for the wife of a prick with sticky fingers.

MARGE. Yes.

ISAAC. Well, that's New York. I mean, that's the ultimate. Wonderful. Let me tell you. I came from the worst place. People turning one another in for a hustle, for a piece of ass, for a piece of black bread, whatever. You get it, sweetie? I mean, if they thought you were a Jew, or not. *Or not.* If they were just pissed off at you 'cause you slighted them. But, this city wins on points. You got me? This city wins on points. Because you had a hard-on to see a crony of your crooked husband? Because you were a little lonely, a little weepy for the old days? You come here, raising the lefty flag—you self-righteous, social-worker-tootsie. Tell me, are you going to put in your report to social services that you came here for a vodka and a flirt fifteen fucking years ago? You're going to tell them that at social services? Hey, let me tell you something, *that* was my wife who did the fundraisers. She dragged every downtrodden threadbare cause into this house, from the Panthers on. And now I should pay 'cause you're bitter? (*Pause.*) Please go home and tell them, go home to your little Smith-Corona and type up, "He's got delusions of persecution, and he's probably gonna end up like Schwartz, dead."

MARGE. Who? End up like ...?

ISAAC. Delmore Schwartz. He said, "Even paranoids have enemies." He used to come here for dinner before he died in the hallway of his hotel. So arbeit does indeed macht frei, huh?

MARGE. I made a horrible mistake.

ISAAC. What in the world could you possibly think I had to do with your husband? It seems positively lunatic to me. Revenge! My God! You came for revenge!

MARGE. What about you? You don't know anything about revenge?

ISAAC. What are you talking about? What do you mean?

MARGE. Your children! "Every day I don't see him is a victory!" "The Neville Chamberlain of sons!" "Fuck them." You could tell me a whole hell of a lot about revenge, Mr. Geldhart.

ISAAC. Revenge I know.

MARGE. Seems to me revenge is the only thing keeping you alive. I don't walk around Manhattan with a grudge. I don't walk around this city thinking of revenge. It just wells up.

ISAAC. That I understand.

MARGE. But I get out of bed, as bad as it gets. I'm not saying I don't have days where I don't get out of bed. I think I spent most of '88 staring up at my ceiling. But I try, I put one foot in front of the other and—most of the time I don't even know why. I just do it. I just do it. Well, I've got to go.

ISAAC. Miss Hackett, may I ask you to have dinner with me?

MARGE. What are you talking about? You want to have dinner? You kicked me out a minute ago, or don't you remember?

ISAAC. I am a forgiving man.

MARGE. What, you want to sit somewhere? You want to go somewhere and sit at a table?

ISAAC. I think it would be very nice, very good, were we to have dinner.

MARGE. No. That would be crossing a line.

ISAAC. They wouldn't know.

MARGE. I'd get canned. No, worse. I'd have a "letter" put in my personal file.

ISAAC. Listen, they don't follow you around. They wouldn't know. What's the big deal? I still have my Diner's Club Card that hasn't been shredded. Gramercy Park has become decent, restaurant-wise. Food is better now than when we were young. No more sauerbraten and schnitzel. You see, there was a time, emigration let some Italians in in the '70s—they brought with them significant secrets.

MARGE. I don't think so.

ISAAC. I would say that professionalism has already been blown.

MARGE. Nevertheless. We just can't have dinner. I can't start doing this sort of thing, I just can't.

ISAAC. Late in the game for romance?

MARGE. Romance is not even a consideration.

ISAAC. Out of your vocabulary? Well, too bad. Maybe you've had all the human traffic a person can bear.

MARGE. Maybe I have. I look at you and it doesn't look so great for you either.

ISAAC. Tell me, then, what chance do you think you have in this world? I am curious?

MARGE. What do you mean, "chance"?

ISAAC. Yes. "Chance." Exactly. What're you going to do? Wait for a better deal?

MARGE. I'm not waiting for anything. In the last five years I put myself through school and got this job, which, admittedly is not what I imagined, but still. What have you *done*, lately? I had to drive out to Long Island with a suit for my husband, because he was wearing jogging pants and a Drexel Burnham tee-shirt when they found him. (*Pause.*) What chance do I have? Fuck you. Man, I hope I don't look fragile or give the impression that I'm on some sort of widow's walk. I have a son who knows his father ripped off everything in this city that wasn't nailed down! I watched my husband on news at five, *weeping*. Chance? What chance do I have? Because I won't have dinner with you? (*Beat.*) Do you know how much I hate having dinner by myself night after night? Well, I'd rather do that, let me assure you, than have dinner with you and compare bad-break notes.

ISAAC. Why? Afraid you're going to see yourself in me? Is that it?

MARGE. We are nothing alike. Whatever has happened to you, you've done to yourself. You had everything and you threw it away.

ISAAC. I threw nothing away.

MARGE. Then this is how you thought your life would go?

ISAAC. You can't even imagine. You have no idea. This is not how I saw my life turn out. But surprised I am not, Miss Hackett. I did this to myself? You don't see any other survivors in your files, do you? You don't see any brothers and sisters? Betrayal? I never even smelt it coming until the fucking *maid* turned us in. The *maid*. She was like my mother, and let me tell you—I don't have self-pity! You don't see a tattoo on my wrist, do you? But they got my grandparents, they got my mother and father, and they got ... I came here to make a family and they trashed it, they got it.

MARGE. I am sorry. But really, I am going to leave.

ISAAC. Listen to me. You came here with an agenda, but now at least listen to what was taken away from me. (*Pause.*) I loved my children. I sure don't love them now. You walk into this house ... (*HE points to a table.*) Aaron cut his head on the tip of that table and I carried him to NYU Hospital when he was two. (*Beat.*) Sarah got laid for the first time in this house, and I thought I was quite literally going to die. (*Beat.*) My wife found this sofa in Kingston and we had it carted down and we sat on it, and it was the most perfect ... my wife ... my wife ... my wife. (*Beat.*) My Martin. He comes in here from Lacrosse when he was sixteen, sneezing, and the next thing, he was, just like that—no blood count at all. (*Beat.*) I sleep now in the living room, because the bedrooms are too much to bear. (*Beat.*) I am so stupid, Miss Hackett, I thought that if I published Hazlitt and Svevo, I'd be spared. The silence, Miss Hackett. The silence. Pointless.

MARGE. (*Thinks before speaking.*) I could never bear to play on my husband's connections. There were people who actually liked him, held a degree of sympathy for him. Because, mainly, he kept quiet. He had a thief's honor. I am owed favors. Specifically. I suppose, I am actually owed *one* favor. The way these things work. Because there are people in this town who actually think my husband *told* me things. Which is rich. (*Beat.*) But. I can make a call. I can call a judge. And they'll just drop it. Like that. And believe me, there'd be nothing your son can do.

ISAAC. Wouldn't that make you just like your husband?

MARGE. No—that's too damn tough, that's just too hard. We're just flesh and blood here. That's all we are. (*Beat.*) Hey, I'm offering you a good hand. What are you gonna do? Wait for a "better deal"? There are so few breaks.

ISAAC. (*After a moment.*) There are, that's true. (*Beat.*) Perhaps you're right. (*Tired.*) I *would* like a break.

MARGE. Then it'll be over.

ISAAC. Over? That would be lovely, if it were over. (*HE picks up the postcard.*) Look at this thing. The man fancied himself a serious artist. Lugging his little brushes about Vienna, God knows. Scraggly hair, greasy. Look at it Look at the sky. When you pick it up, to think of where it's been ... what the day was like when he made it. (*Lost for an instant, soft.*) All the things to come. So much to come.

MARGE. It's just a lousy postcard. My husband had post-it notes all over the place, and I didn't save them.

ISAAC. (*Looking at her with a great, sudden affection.*) Goddamn it, it's a pity I could not persuade you to dine with me. I can be amusing. Especially when I take the anti-depressants they prescribe. Then I am at my best. Restaurants are so hard to bear alone.

MARGE. You do not have to eat alone. (*SHE looks at him for a moment. And turns to exit.*)

ISAAC. Miss Hackett? Thank you. Maybe, when the time is more appropriate ... maybe when the weather turns kinder, we *could* have dinner.

MARGE. That ... would be nice, Isaac. Good night. (*SHE exits.*)

(*ISAAC picks up postcard, and then, sets it alight. Placing it in an ashtray, HE sits looking at it. Snow streams down. The card burns. After a moment, MARTIN enters.*)

MARTIN. She left.
ISAAC. She left. Yes. She's gone, she went.
MARTIN. What is that? What are you doing?
ISAAC. Nothing.

(*Beat.*)

MARTIN. How was it?

ISAAC. Well, you can relax for a while. You won't have to write my checks and listen to complaints of the cook and make sure that my underwear is changed, for a little while yet.

MARTIN. Of course not. I know that.

ISAAC. So you can relax, you're free.

MARTIN. Well I wouldn't mind. I'd do it.

ISAAC. You would. Yes, you would. Why wouldn't you mind, Martin? I don't understand ... why you wouldn't mind after this ...?

MARTIN. Because I am not, unfortunately, as strong as you.

ISAAC. What does that mean? Martin? Please? What?

MARTIN. I don't know. I don't have it in me to do this thing that you do: resolving to write people off, to write it all off. I don't. Believe me, I've tried.

ISAAC. And now what're you—you're going back upstate?

MARTIN. There's a train in forty minutes, yeah. But they're all backed up. So, it's good that it worked out with the ... Look, you call if you want anything. I'll be up there tonight.

(Silence.)

ISAAC. Maybe I'll walk outside with you a bit. It's so lovely with the snow. Do you want to walk through the park?

MARTIN. Sure.

ISAAC. I need to find the key to the park. Let me find the key.

MARTIN. Wait. I've still got mine.

(MARTIN puts on his coat, hands ISAAC his. THEY walk out to the hall. MARTIN turns off the light.)

THE END

COSTUME PLOT

ISAAC
ACT I:
Double-breasted dark blue suit (2 piece)
White shirt
Snakeskin belt
Blue tie with beige figures
Dark blue dress socks with maroon & beige designs
Black straight tip tie shoes
ACT II:
Distressed & wrinkled charcoal gray 2-piece suit
Un-ironed white shirt
Black belt
Maroon tie with figures
Old straight tip tie shoes
Black figured socks
Charcoal gray ill-fitting jacket (preset)
Charcoal gray overcoat
MARTIN
ACT I:
Tweed sports jacket
Khaki twill pants
Brown belt
Green print shirt
Black suede shoes with heavy rubber soles
Khaki socks
Glasses
Watch
ACT II:
Olive corduroy pants

Denim work shirt
Red & black pullover sweater
Brown belt
Work boots
Khaki socks
Glasses
Khaki poplin outer jacket
Tweed and fur cap with earflaps & visor
Black leather gloves
Watch
SARAH
ACT I:
Lightweight rose print mid-calf length skirt
Beige shirt/blouse with rose 1/4 ribbon bow
White figured socks
Ankle length brown boots with laces & 2-inch heels
Watch
Earrings
AARON
ACT I:
Gray/green 2 pc. suit
White shirt with brown stripes
Suspenders
Maroon tie with figures
Black wing tip loafers
Maroon paisley socks
Watch
MARGE HACKETT
ACT II:
Purple suede skirt
Beige sweater (tucked in)

Blue & purple long, thin silk scarf
Black coat
Shawl overcoat
Black bag
Stockings
Calf-high boots with heels
Soft hart (carries on)
Watch

PROPERTY PLOT

ACT I:
Conference table with four chairs
Round side table for coffee DR
Chair UR
Small square table DL for manuscripts and pencils
Chair DL
2 trays : one for mugs, one for thermoses, etc.
2 coffee thermoses
1 mug with stir straws
1 creamer with milk
1 sugar bowl with sugar cubes
5 napkins
6 coffee mugs
4 Rising Tide manuscripts by Val Chenard
8 misc. manuscripts
Pencil cup with pens and pencils
Ashtray
Atlas of the Holocaust books
Destruction of the Sephardim books
Hobson-Jobson manuscript
Sarah's bag with:
    LA Style Magazine
    Wallet
    Filofax
    Plane ticket
    Carmex
    TV script
Highball glass
Teacup and saucer
Martin's backpack

Martin's cigarettes and lighter
ACT II:
Sofa
Tall table behind sofa
Coffee table
UL armchair
CL armchair
DR armchair
DR side table
Magazines, newspapers and bills scattered on floor
Boxes—book boxes and file boxes
Keys
Silver tray
2 decanters
4 highball glasses
2 dirty china cups with saucers
One china plate with leftover sacher torte
Ice bucket
Ashtray
Fancy lighter
Radio
Blanket
"Childhood, Youth, and Exile"book
The Geldhart Collection
Several portfolios
One portfolio with Illustrated letters[*]
One portfolio with Hitler postcard
Marge's briefcase with:

---

[*] Located in "The Illustrated Letter" by Charles Hamilton published by Universe Books. This book also contains a copy of the real Hitler postcard.

Clipboard
Questionnaire
Pen
Notebook
Cigarettes
Backup lighter

THE NORMAL HEART

(Advanced Groups.) Drama. Larry Kramer. 8m., 1f. Unit set. The New York Shakespeare Festival had quite a success with this searing drama about public and private indifference to the Acquired Immune Deficiency Syndrome plague, commonly called AIDS, and about one man's lonely fight to wake the world up to the crisis. The play has subsequently been produced to great acclaim in London and Los Angeles. Brad Davis originated the role of Ned Weeks, a gay activist enraged at the foot-dragging of both elected public officials and the gay community itself regarding AIDS. Ned not only is trying to save the world from itself, he also must confront the personal toll of AIDS when his lover contracts the disease and ultimately dies. This is more than just a gay play about a gay issue. This is a public health issue which affects all of us. He further uses this theatrical platform to plead with gay brethren to stop thinking of themselves only in terms of their sexuality, and that rampant sexual promiscuity will not only almost guarantee that they will contract AIDS; it is also bad for them as human beings. "An angry, unremitting and gripping piece of political theatre."—N.Y. Daily News. "Like the best social playwright, Kramer produces a cross-fire of life and death energies that illuminate the many issues and create a fierce and moving human drama."—Newsweek. $4.50. (Royalty $60-$40.) Slightly Restricted. (#788)

A QUIET END

(Adult Groups.) Drama. Robin Swados. 5m. Int. Three men—a schoolteacher, an aspiring jazz pianist and an unemployed actor—have been placed in a run-down Manhattan apartment. All have lost their jobs, all have been shunned by their families, and all have AIDS. They have little in common, it seems, apart from their slowing evolving, albeit uneasy, friendships with each other, and their own mortality. The interaction of the men with a psychiatrist (heard but not seen throughout the course of the play) and the entrance into this arena of the ex-lover of one of the three—seemingly healthy, yet unsure of his future—opens up the play's true concerns: the meaning of friendship, loyalty and love. By celebrating the lives of four men who, in the face of death, become more fearlessly life-embracing instead of choosing the easier path to a quiet end, the play explores the human side of the AIDS crisis, examining how we choose to lead our lives—and how we choose to end them. "The play, as quiet in its message as in its ending, gets the measure of pain and love in a bitter-chill climate."—N.Y. Post. "In a situation that will be recognizable to most gay people, it is the chosen family rather than the biological family, that has become important to these men. Robin Swados has made an impressive debut with A Quiet End by accurately representing the touching relationships in such a group."—N.Y. Native. (Royalty $60-$40.) Music Note: Samuel French, Inc. can supply a cassette tape of music from the original New York production, composed by Robin Swados, upon receipt of a refundable deposit of $25.00, (tape must be returned within one week from the close of your production) and a rental fee of $15.00 per performance. Use of this music in productions is optional. (#19017)

Other Publications for Your Interest

BENEFACTORS
(LITTLE THEATRE—COMIC DRAMA)
By MICHAEL FRAYN

2 men, 2 women—Interior

Do not expect another *Noises Off*; here the multi-talented Mr. Frayn has more on his mind than Just Plain Fun. *Benefactors*, a long-running Broadway and London hit, is about doing good and do-gooding (not the same) and about the way the world changes outside your control just when you are trying to change it yourself. The story concerns an architect who has the sixties notion that if you give people good environments they will be good people. But, given a South London development to design, he is forced by town planners to go for a high-rise, characterless scheme. No sooner does he begin to believe in this scheme than the fashion for high rises goes bust. ". . . one of the subtlest plays Broadway has seen in years, by one of the most extraordinary writers of the English-speaking theater . . . more political than most political plays, more intimate than most intimate plays and wiser than almost any play around today."—Newsweek. ". . . a fine . . . very good play . . . A Christmas present for theatergoers."—WABC-TV. ". . . a high point of the theater season . . . rare wit and intelligence."—Wall Street Journal. ". . . fascinating and astonishing play . . ."—N.Y. Daily News. ". . . dazzling and devastating play . . ."—N.Y. Times. ". . . a tour de force . . . simultaneously compelling and alienating . . ."—Christian Science Monitor.   (#3980)

PACK OF LIES
(LITTLE THEATRE—DRAMA)
By HUGH WHITEMORE

3 men, 5 women—Combination interior

Bob and Barbara Jackson are a nice middle-aged English couple. Their best friends are their neighbors, Helen and Peter Kroger, who are Canadian. All is blissful in the protected, contained little world of the Jacksons; until, that is, a detective from Scotland Yard asks if his organization may use the Jackson's house as an observation station to try and foil a Soviet spy ring operating in the area. Being Good Citizens the Jacksons oblige, though they become progressively more and more put out as Scotland Yard's demands on them increase. They are really put to the test when the detective reveals to them that the spies are, in fact, their best friends the Krogers. Scotland Yard asks the Jacksons to cooperate with them to trap the spies, which really puts the Jacksons on the horns of a dilemma. Do they have the right to "betray" their friends? "This is a play about the morality of lying, not the theatrics of espionage, and, in Mr. Whitemore's view, lying is a virulent disease that saps patriots and traitors alike of their humanity."—N.Y. Times. "A crackling melodrama."—Wall St. Journal. "Absolutely engrossing . . . an evening of dynamic theatre."—N.Y. Post. "A superior British drama."—Chr. Sci. Mon.   (#18154)

Other Publications for Your Interest

A MAP OF THE WORLD
(ADVANCED GROUPS—DRAMA)
By DAVID HARE

7 men, 4 women, plus extras—2 Interiors

This new play by the author of *Plenty* "is an ambitious work which brings together in heated discussion a young left wing journalist and a right wing expatriate Indian novelist. The settings are a Bombay hotel where they are attending a world poverty conference and the British film studio where the Indian author's experiences are being turned into a film. Throughout the play, life and fiction overlap . . . One of the issues is the sexual jealousy that arises over the men's competition for the favours of a promiscuous American actress staying at the hotel. Also on the agenda: idealism vs. cynicism; the West's arrogance in its handling of Third World problems; the alleged evils of Zionism; and the journalist's fervent belief in the necessity for change."—London Sunday Express. "It is a pleasure to hear a stage echoing to such issues and such talk."—London Standard. "A rich and complex play built around a series of antitheses: the Third World and the West, fiction and reality, irony and committment, reason and passion, the personal and the political. Yet for me what makes it the most mature and moving of Hare's works to date is its gut conviction that once we lose our Utopian dreams we have lost everything."—London Guardian.   (#15620)

NANAWATAI
(ADVANCED GROUPS—DRAMA)
By WILLIAM MASTROSIMONE

10 men, 1 woman, plus chorus of female extras—Unit set

The intrepid Mr. Mastrosimone, heretofore the author of studies of character such as *The Woolgatherer*, *A Tantalizing*, *Shivaree* and *Extremities*, has here set his sights on an epic scale. Shortly after the Soviet Union invaded Afghanistan, Mr. Mastrosimone managed to get himself smuggled into that beleaguered country via Pakistan. There he spent several weeks with the Afghani rebels, observing their often futile attempts to resist the Russian blitzkrieg. All of the resistance he witnessed was not futile, though; he also observed the capture and execution of a Soviet tank crew. It was this incident which inspired *Nanawatai* (an Afghani word which means "sanctuary"). The story is told through the dual points of view of a Russian tank crew member and an Afghani rebel, as a chorus of village women impresses upon us the effect on the citizenry of all the bloodshed (not unlike, of course, in a Greek tragedy). "Hard-hitting and probing . . . alive with issues and conflicts of both a political and personal nature."—Hollywood Reporter. "It has the ritual power of Greek tragedy."—L.A. Times.   (#15975)

Other Publications for Your Interest

EMERALD CITY
(LITTLE THEATRE—COMEDY)

By DAVID WILLIAMSON
(author of the screenplays to "The Year of Living Dangerously" and Gallipoli")

3 men, 3 women—Unit set

In "the trade"—i.e., the movie biz as covered by *Variety*—"Oz" is not over the rainbow but Down Under. Australia. Which makes Sydney the Emerald City, where there is not one wizard but a host of them, who are the Deal-Makers. Colin, a critically-praised but commercially under-successful screenwriter, and his wife Kate, an Editor, feel a change of venue is called for, from Melbourne (i.e., The Sticks) to Sydney, the Emerald City, the major leagues. There, Colin joins forces with an aggressive, fast-talking aspiring screen-writer named Mike, who has no discernible talent for writing but who is a genius at the Art of the Deal. Mike parlays his tenuous connection with Colin into a series of cinematic projects which culminate in his becoming a global tycoon, a pinnacle from which he can put many different projects into "development", such as Kate's pet project, a serious ab-original novel, which Mike plans to transplant to Tennessee as a vehicle for Eddie Murphy. Eventually, Colin and Kate must make a moral decision: is the Emerald City a sane place to be: or do they want to go back to Kansas? "Hype and Hypocrisy amusingly help to speed the plow on the road to *Emerald City*."—N.Y. Times. "Winsomely cynical."—Time Mag. "Funny and engaging...his characters must be as much fun to play as they are to listen to." —N.Y. Post. "An incisive, grimly graceful, painfully funny play...this examination of how the noble ambition for fame deteriorates into lust for money and power, and how relation-ships of every kind subsist on deception, deserves our delightedly undivided attention. *Emerald City* portrays human rivalry with maximum comic and dramatic effect because it is as humorous as it is witty."—N.Y. Mag.

(#7078)

THE FILM SOCIETY
(LITTLE THEATRE—DRAMATIC COMEDY

By JON ROBIN BAITZ

4 men, 2 women—Various interiors. (may be unit set).

Imagine the best of Simon Gray crossed with the best of Athol Fugard. The New York critics lavished praise upon this wonderful play, calling Mr. Baitz a major new voice in our theatre. *The Film Society*, set in South Africa, is *not* about the effects of apartheid—at least, overtly. Blenheim is a provincial private school modeled on the second-rate British education machine. It is 1970, a time of complacency for everyone but Terry, a former teacher at Blenheim, who has lost his job because of his connections with Blacks (he invited a Black priest to speak at Commencement). Terry tries to involve Jonathan, another teacher at the school and the central character in this play; but Jonathan cares only about his film society, which he wants to keep going at all costs—even if it means programming only safe, non-objectionable, films. When Jonathan's mother, a local rich lady, promises to donate a substantial amount of money to Blenheim if Jonathan is made Headmaster, he must finally choose which side he is on: Terry's or The Establishment's. "Using the school of a microcosm for South Africa, Baitz explores the psychological workings of repression in a society that has to kill its conscience in order to persist in a course of action it knows enough to abhor but cannot afford to relinquish."—New Yorker. "What distinguishes Mr. Baitz' writing, aside from its manifest literacy, is its ability to em-brace the ambiguities of political and moral dilemmas that might easily be reduced to blacks and whites."—N.Y. Times. "A beautiful, accomplished play...things I thought I was a churl still to value or expect—things like character, plot and theatre dialogue—really do matter."—N.Y. Daily News.

(#8123)

Other Publications for Your Interest

DOMINO
(ADVANCED GROUPS—COMIC DRAMA)
By ROBERT LITZ

6 men, 1 woman to play various roles/Unit Set.

This "excruciatingly funny political comedy" (N.Y. Post) is about a rather thick U.S. foreign loan banker who visits a Central American banana republic, supervised by a charmingly cynical C.I.A. operative, to renegotiate a 3.8 billion dollar debt. Unwittingly, he winds up financing and mastermining the overthrow of the government. Written in short, hilarious scenes (well, "hilarious" in a rather frightening way...) *Domino* has a lot to tell us about what what is really going on in these days of Contras, Sandinistas and Noriegas. "Hostages are taken; prisoners are tortured; ransoms are paid; weapons are hijacked; drugs are traded; political deals are struck—and press conferences are held to celebrate the whole sordid mess. Then, when the C.I.A. discovers a more expedient way to sell off the country to capitalist interests, everybody betrays everybody else, and the whole cycle is played all over again. After a while you can't tell the corrupt generals from the bought-out guerillas. And if there ever was a hero, or an honest idealist, in the house, somebody shot him."—N.Y. Post. $4.00

(#6165)

EL SALVADOR
(LITTLE THEATRE—DRAMA)
By RAFAEL LIMA

6 men, 1 woman—Interior.

This brilliant new naturalistic drama from NYC's famed Circle Repertory takes place in a hotel room in El Salvador which has been converted into a home base for a dissolute and mostly disillusioned gaggle of U.S. TV journalists, fed up with the futility of constantly risking their lives reporting on a revolution that nobody back home cares about. Not that *they* care much, either—but it does give them something to talk about. The play takes place on a day when the El Salvador military, flying sophisticated helicopters provided them by the U.S. government, have bombed a small remote village, killing many civilians, including women and children. That night, as they wait out an attack on the capital and, possibly, on the hotel, the crew members talk of their feelings about the war, their shame about America's role in it, and their separation from loved ones far away. "A tensely fascinating evening in the theatre."—N.Y. Post. "*The Front Page* transposed to a Third World war zone."—Village Voice. "A powerful, gripping drama...has the ring of authenticity that is as vivid as reality. You are absolutely there."—UPI. "Lima knows his subject and has illuminated it with pungent dialogue and crackling theatricalism."—N.Y. Daily News.

(#7024)

Other Publications for Your Interest

OTHER PEOPLE'S MONEY
(LITTLE THEATRE—DRAMA)

By JERRY STERNER

3 men, 2 women—One Set

Wall Street takeover artist Lawrence Garfinkle's intrepid computer is going "tilt" over the undervalued stock of New England Wire & Cable. He goes after the vulnerable company, buying up its stock to try and take over the company at the annual meeting. If the stockholders back Garfinkle, they will make a bundle—but what of the 1200 employees? What of the local community? Too bad, says Garfinkle, who would then liquidate the company—take the money and run. Set against the charmingly rapacious financier are Jorgenson, who has run the company since the Year One and his chief operations officer, Coles, who understands, unlike the genial Jorgenson, what a threat Garfinkle poses to the firm. They bring in Kate, a bright young woman lawyer, who specializes in fending off takeovers—and who is the daughter of Jorgenson's administrative assistant, Bea. Kate must not only contend with Garfinkle—she must also move Jorgenson into taking decisive action. Should they use "greenmail"? Try to find a "White Knight"? Employ a "shark repellent"? This compelling drama about Main Street vs. Wall Street is as topical and fresh as today's headlines, giving its audience an inside look at what's *really going on* in this country and asking trenchant questions, not the least of which is whether a corporate raider is really the creature from the Black Lagoon of capitalism or the Ultimate Realist come to save business from itself.

(#17064)

THE DOWNSIDE
(LITTLE THEATRE—COMEDY)

By RICHARD DRESSER

6 men, 2 women—Combination Interior

These days, American business is a prime target for satire, and no recent play has cut as deep, with more hilarious results, than this superb new comedy from the Long Wharf Theatre, Mark & Maxwell, a New Jersey pharmaceuticals firm, has acquired U.S. rights to market an anti-stress drug manufactured in Europe, pending F.D.A. approval; but the marketing executives have got to come up with a snazzy ad campaign by January—and here we are in December! The irony is that nowhere is this drug more needed than right there at Mark & Maxwell, a textbook example of corporate ineptitude, where it seems all you have to do to get ahead is look good in a suit. The marketing strategy meetings get more and more pointless and frenetic as the deadline approaches. These meetings are "chaired" by Dave, the boss, who is never actually there—he is a voice coming out of a box, as Dave phones in while jetting to one meeting or another, eventually directing the ad campaign on his mobile phone while his plane is being hijacked! Doesn't matter to Dave, though—what matters is the possible "downside" of this new drug: hallucinations. "Ridiculous", says the senior marketing executive Alan: who then proceeds to tell how Richard Nixon comes to his house in the middle of the night to visit . . . "Richard Dresser's deft satirical sword pinks the corporate image repeatedly, leaving the audience amused but thoughtful."—Meriden Record. "Funny and ruthlessly cynical."—Phila. Inquirer. "A new comedy that is sheer delight."—Westport News. "The Long Wharf audience laughed a lot, particularly those with office training. But they were also given something to ponder about the way we get things done in America these days, or rather pretend to get things done. No wonder the Japanese are winning."—L.A. Times.

(#6718)